Matthew S. Armstrong

Jane & Mizmow

HARPER

An Imprint of HarperCollins*Publishers*

Jane's best friend is Mizmow.

Mizmow's best friend is Jane.

But it can be hard being best friends with a monster.
Mizmow loves to climb trees.

Jane would rather keep both feet on the ground.

Jane loves the seesaw.

Mizmow does too.

In the fall, it's Jane's job to rake the leaves.
Then she gets to jump in them.

Mizmow helps—especially with the red ones. They taste best.

But they are still best friends.
Jane shares her books with Mizmow.

Mizmow shares his snacks with Jane.

Jane helps Mizmow at bathtime.

Mizmow keeps Jane's feet warm at night.

And on the first chilly day of the year, they both love to wear a warm cap fresh from the dryer.

Mizmow is mad.

Jane is more mad.

They say sorry.

But it doesn't work. They are not best friends anymore.

Bathtime isn't fun.

There is no one to share snacks with.

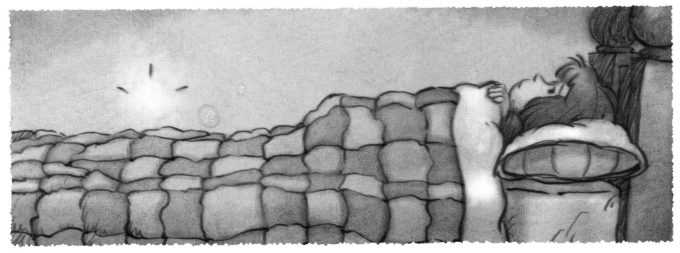

Jane can't fall asleep. Her feet are too cold.

And Mizmow misses sharing books with Jane. They just don't taste the same without her.

Still, Jane is fine all by herself. . . .

So is Mizmow. He finds a new friend.

How can you get your best friend back?

Mizmow has an idea.

So does Jane.

Jane will never be able to rake up all of those leaves.

Luckily, she has some help.

"My hero," says Jane.
"But even better—

my friend!"

for Isabelle

Library of Congress Cataloging-in-Publication Data.   Armstrong, Matthew S.   Jane & Mizmow / by Matthew S. Armstrong. — 1st ed.   p. cm.   Summary: Jane and her best friend, a monster named Mizmow, are best friends in spite of their differences, and nothing can keep them apart.   ISBN 978-0-06-117719-4 (trade bdg.) — ISBN 978-0-06-117720-0 (lib. bdg.) [1. Best friends—Fiction. 2. Friendship—Fiction. 3. Monsters—Fiction.] I. Title. PZ7.A73376Ja 2011   2010012628   [E]—dc22   CIP   AC
Typography by Dana Fritts.   11 12 13 14 15 SCP   10 9 8 7 6 5 4 3 2 1 ❖ First Edition